BOLD KIDS

MW01152090

Tennessee

CHILDREN'S AMERICAN LOCAL HISTORY BOOK

Facts about Tennessee for kids is a great way to teach your child about the state's history, culture, and landmarks. With a picture of the state flag and fun trivia, this book will keep your kids engaged and entertained while doing their homework.

Whether your child is just starting to learn about the state, or you're looking to give your teacher an idea for an upcoming project, this fact sheet is a great way to teach them about the state of music!

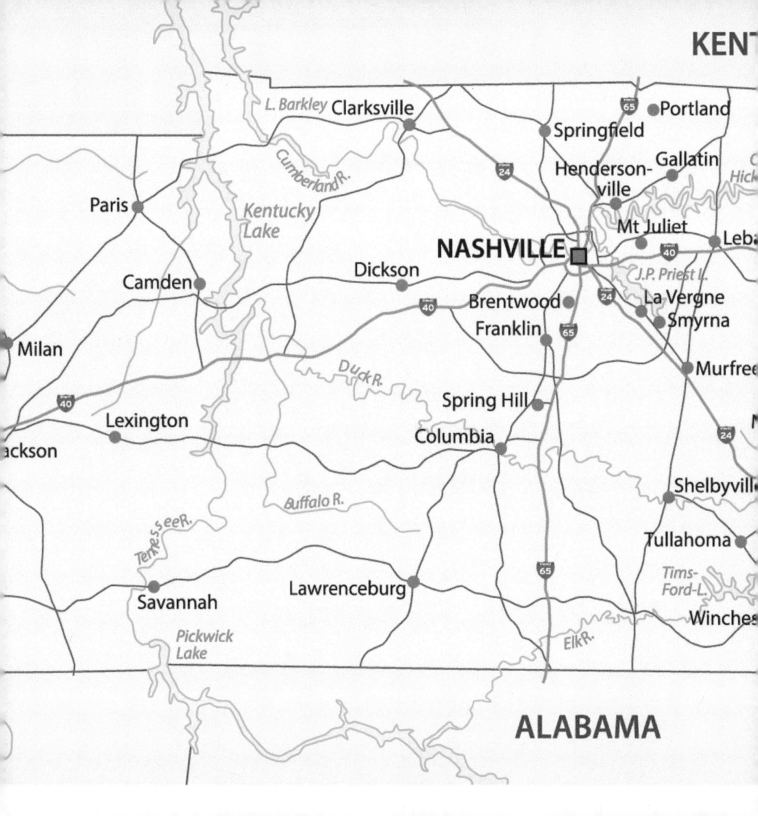

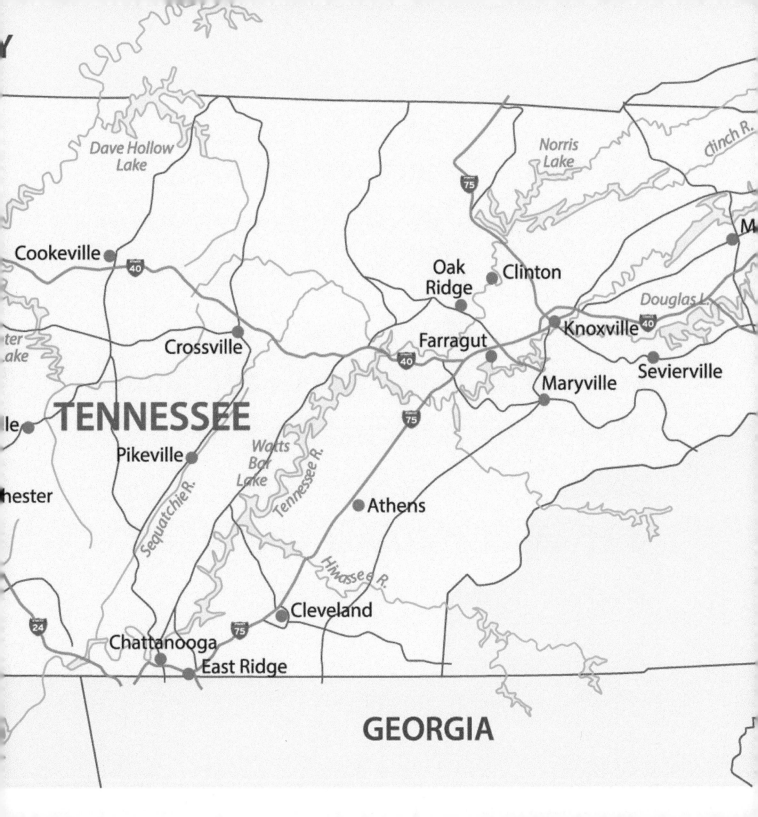

There are several fun facts about Tennessee for kids. These can also be expanded upon to cover other interesting facts about the state. You can teach your child about the Great Smoky Mountains National Park or about the country's culture with a study of Nashville and other popular tourist destinations.

A notebook that features all 50 states will help your children learn more about each state. You can also use Facts about the state for a unit study on the 50 states.

You can also include some fun facts about Tennessee for kids by incorporating some fun activities into your curriculum. The Great Smoky Mountains are one of the most popular destinations in the US. You can even learn about its natural history by visiting the Great Smoky Mountains national park.

You can make a simple autumn tree with handprints and Q-tips. You can even include fun facts about the state's famous people such as Elvis Presley and Miranda Lambert.

Tennessee is home to many celebrities and country music stars, so be sure to share this with your kids. They can even make their own paper straw puppets to play with. Afterwards, they can read a picture book about the state that is all about honey bees.

If you have a few minutes to spare, you can even create a lesson about the importance of honey bees. A book of this nature can be a great way to learn about the importance of bees to agriculture.

If you're a parent and want to learn more about the state, try these facts about Tennessee for kids. The information will not only provide fun facts about the state, but will also provide valuable information for your child.

The great SMoky Mountains and the country's capital, Nashville, are both worth a visit. Besides being an amazing destination, there are many other interesting things to know about Tennessee. The most well-known is the state's nickname, Volunteer State.

The state is an ideal place for children to learn about the Great Smoky Mountains and other important landmarks. There are also many great historical museums in the state, and the Great Smoky Mountains are among the most popular national parks in the country.

With so much to do and learn, you'll have no problem finding something interesting for your child to learn about. With these Tennessee facts for kids, your children will be captivated by the beauty of the region and the history of this American state.

Apart from the great music and culture of Tennessee, the state is also home to several mountain ranges and has an interesting nickname, Volunteer State. Moreover, the state has more trees per square mile than any other US state.

This makes it an excellent place for families with kids to spend time together and learn about the state's culture. But there are many other interesting facts about Tennessee for kids that you can expand to make your children more knowledgeable.

Despite its small size, Tennessee has a lot of important historical and cultural landmarks. It's also home to the Great Smoky Mountains National Park, which is the largest in the eastern U.S. Its hot, humid summers make the state a hot and humid place.

Nevertheless, this fact sheet is just the beginning of an educational journey about the state of Tennessee for kids. You can always expand on these facts to teach your child about the state's unique history, culture, and geography.

Among its famous citizens are country music stars and celebrities. It also has many mountains, which are the reason for its nickname, Volunteer State. With so many interesting facts about Tennessee for kids, you can make learning fun and exciting.

These worksheets will also help your child learn more about Tennessee and its people. They will enjoy learning about this fascinating state. For their education, try Facts about the state of Tennessee for kids will be an excellent way to teach them more about this fascinating state.

Ingram Content Group UK Ltd.
Milton Keynes UK
UKHW050607200623
423697UK00007B/135